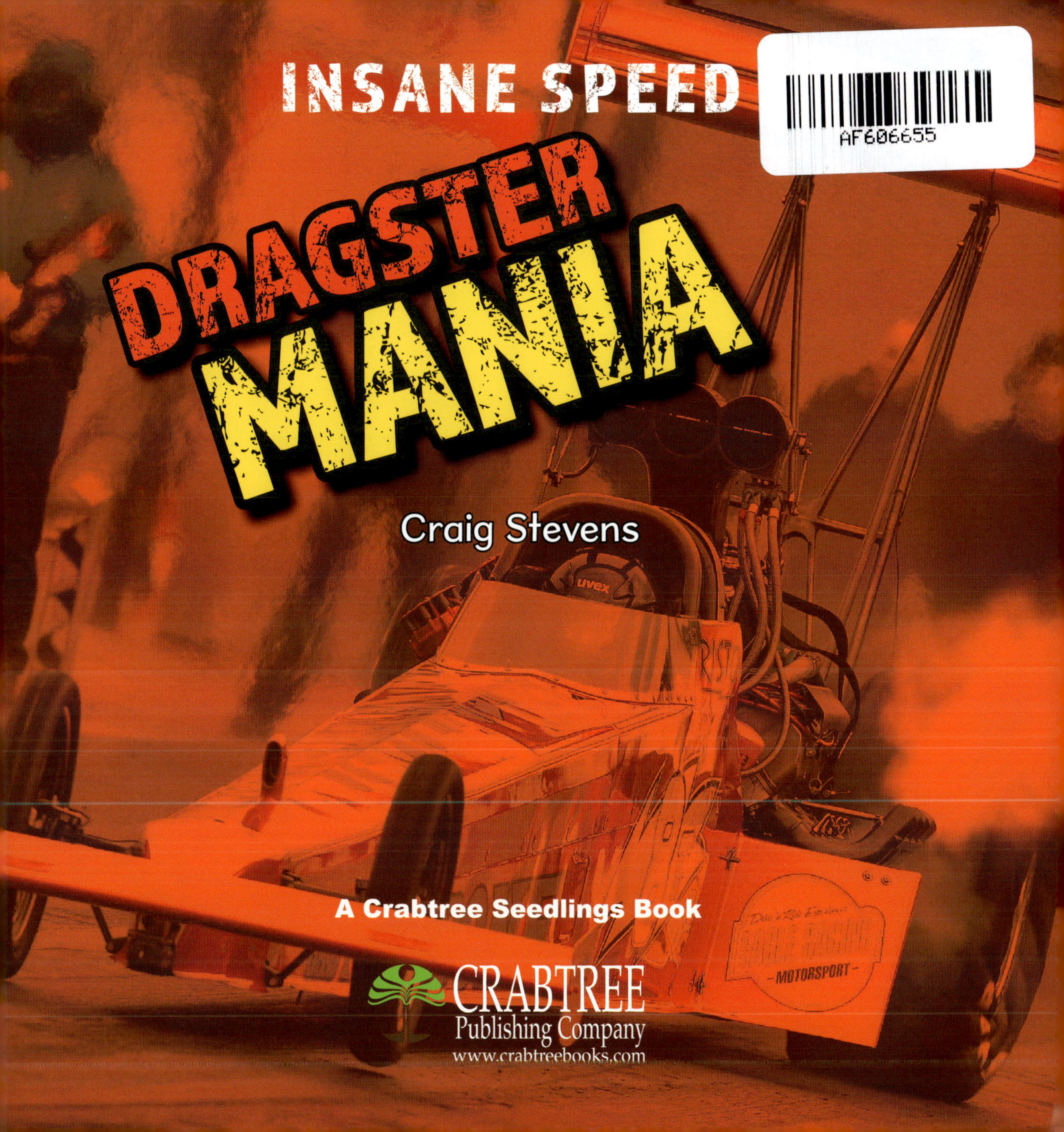
INSANE SPEED
DRAGSTER MANIA
Craig Stevens
A Crabtree Seedlings Book
CRABTREE
Publishing Company
www.crabtreebooks.com
MOTORSPORT
uvex

Coca-Cola
CAMARO
PEAK
COOLANT & MOTOR OIL
AUTO CLUB
CHEVROLET
GOODYEAR
FREIGHTLINER
Advance Auto Parts
STANLEY

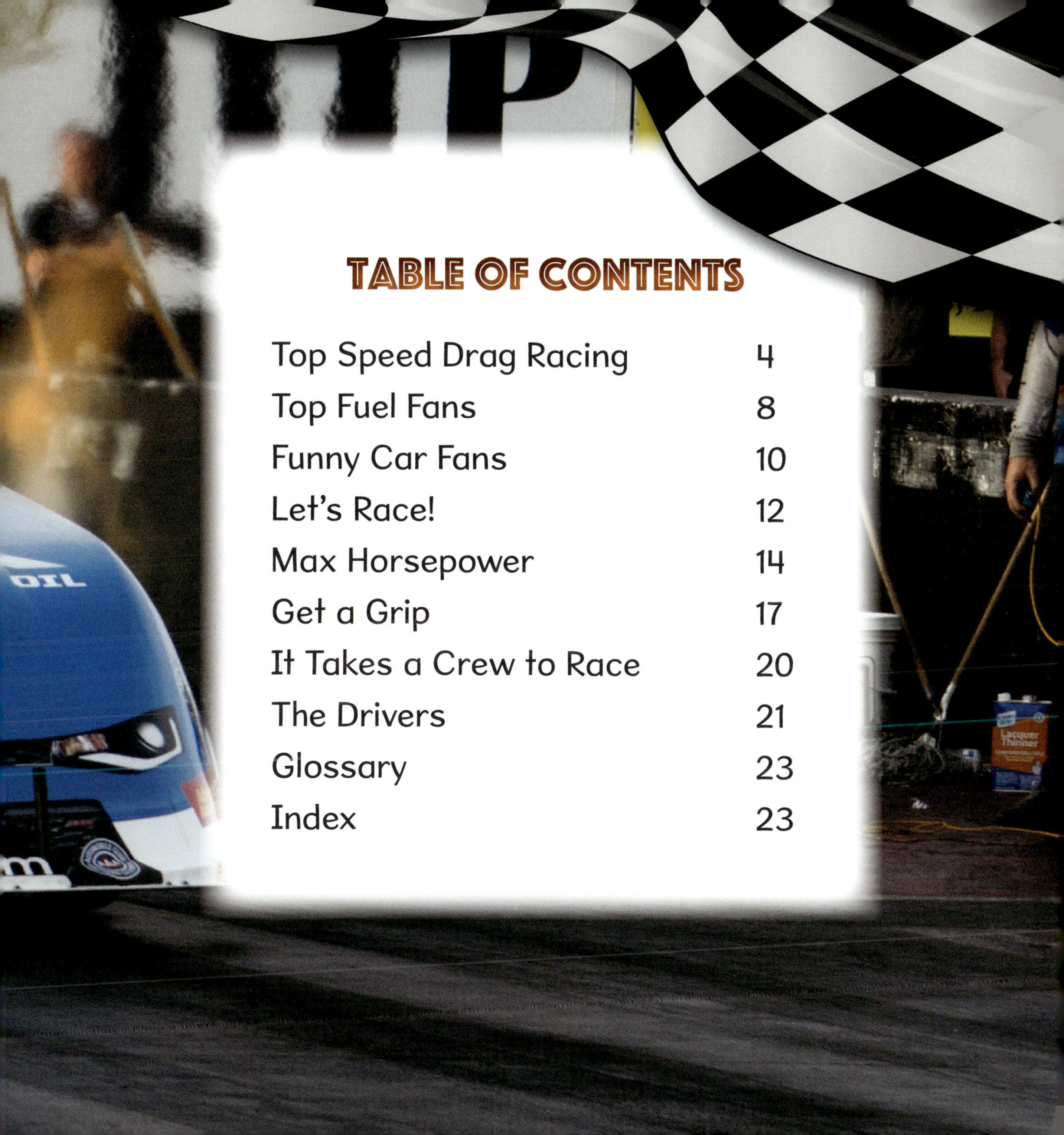

TABLE OF CONTENTS

TOP SPEED DRAG RACING

Drag racing is a motorsport where two cars race down a 1,000-foot (305-meter) straight track to see who can go the fastest.

Top Fuel dragsters race side-by-side at over 300 miles (483 kilometers) per hour.

Top Fuel Dragster

AT THE START OF EACH RACE:

Pre-Stage

- The drivers roll forward until the top lights come on.

Stage

- The drivers roll forward a little more to a sensor. This turns on the yellow lights. They light up one at a time, half a second apart.
- When the green lights come on—the drivers can go!
- If a driver goes before the green lights come on, the red light activates and the countdown is stopped.

Funny Car Dragster

The fastest dragster racing classes are *Top Fuel* and *Funny Car*. These are also the most popular—and for good reason: The cars are the fastest and loudest of all dragsters.

TOP FUEL FANS

Top Fuel fans love the sleek design of this 25-foot (7.5-meter) long racing machine. These cars run faster than Funny Cars because they are lighter.

TOP FUEL FACTS

- Engine in rear of racer
- Weighs about 2,300 pounds (1,043 kilograms)
- Powered by nitromethane
- Exhaust flames can get as hot as 7,000 degrees Fahrenheit (3,871 degrees Celsius)

FUNNY CAR FANS

Funny Car fans love to follow and cheer for their favorite car model. Chevy, Ford, and Dodge automobiles are just a few that are used in drag racing.

FUNNY CAR FACTS

- Engine in front of racer
- Heavier than Top Fuel cars
- Car bodies look similar to road models
- Cannot be older than 5 years

Let's Race!

1. The drivers spin their tires in a burnout to heat them up for a better grip.

2. The drivers pull up to the starting line. This is called staging.

3. The drivers watch for the green light.

4. **OFF YOU GO!**

The cars accelerate to over 300 miles (483 kilometers) per hour in under 5 seconds!

Dragsters go really fast in a short distance. Brakes alone are not powerful enough to stop a dragster. Parachutes are used at the end of the race to slow it down.

MAX HORSEPOWER

Drag racing is all about big engines. Big engines are the force, or **horsepower** (hp), that powers the car down the track at lightning speeds.

Top Fuel and Funny Car dragsters both have similar 500-cubic-inch (8.2 liter) engines. These engines produce over 11,000 hp ...AMAZING!

The engine creates so much heat that mechanics need to rebuild it after each race.

Dragsters do burn-outs to melt the tires making them hot and sticky. This helps the tires grip the track.

The engine has so much power, the tires buckle trying to keep up.

GET A GRIP

All dragsters have "slicks," or smooth rear tires. Smooth tires stick to the track for better **traction** than normal tires, which have a **tread**.

A dragster does a burnout and gets ready to race.

<u>wheelie bar</u> - stops the car from flipping over backward

<u>car body</u> - thin and light

<u>front spoiler</u> - uses the rushing air to keep the front of the car down on the track

engine - provides the power needed to go over 300 miles (483 kilometers) per hour
rear spoiler - uses the rushing air to keep the rear of the car down on the track
cockpit - space where the driver sits
racing slicks - provide grip on the track, helping the car to accelerate
CAPCO
CAPCO
CONTRACTORS INC.
MAC TOOLS

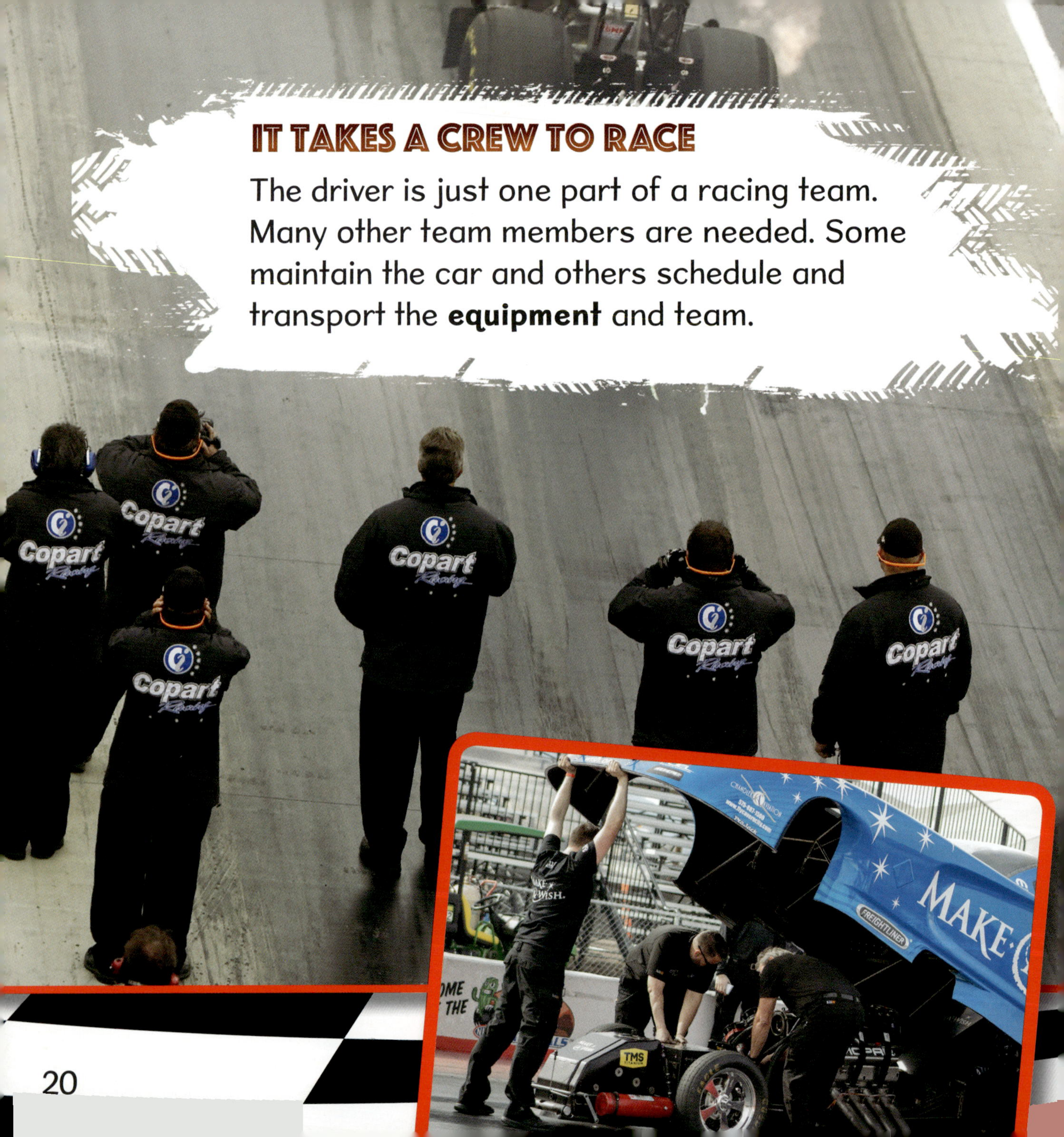

IT TAKES A CREW TO RACE

The driver is just one part of a racing team. Many other team members are needed. Some maintain the car and others schedule and transport the **equipment** and team.

THE DRIVERS

Drag racers wear a helmet and a fireproof suit with a face mask, gloves, socks, and shoes. They sit in the cockpit and wear a quick-release harness, which protects better than a seatbelt at high speeds.

Drag racing is extremely dangerous and the drivers have to be incredibly brave. The speed at which the cars accelerate and **decelerate** puts great force on the driver's body—a bit like riding a super-scary roller coaster!

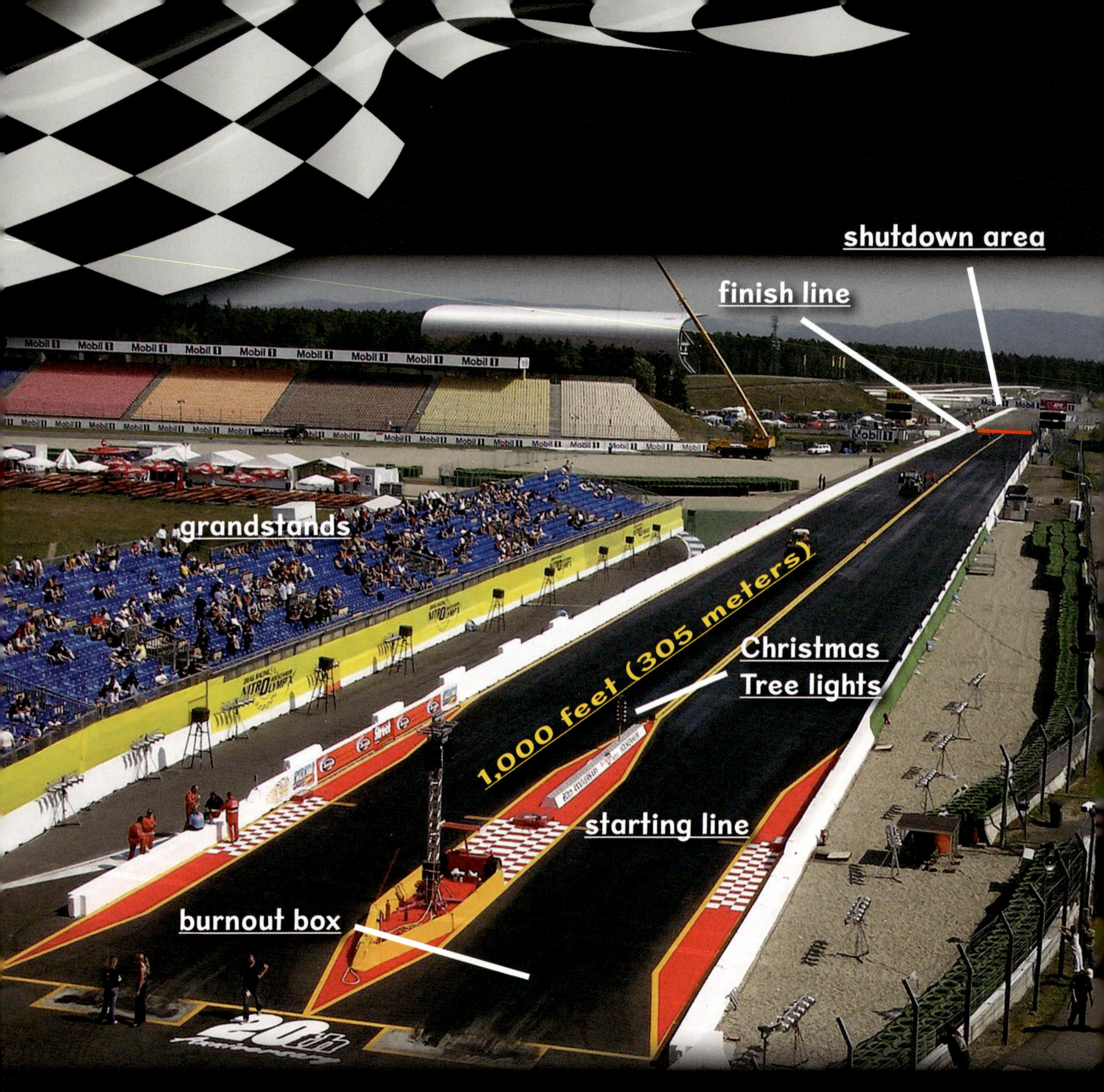
shutdown area
finish line
grandstands
1,000 feet (305 meters)
Christmas Tree lights
starting line
burnout box

Glossary

accelerate (ak-SEL-uh-rayte): Get faster and faster

decelerate (dee-SEL-uh-rayte): Get slower and slower

equipment (uh-KWIP-muhnt): The tools or clothing needed to do a job or play a sport

horsepower (HORS-pow-er): A unit used to measure engine power

traction (TRAK-shuhn): The gripping power of something moving on a surface

tread (TRED): The ridges or bumps on a car tire

Index

School-to-Home Support for Caregivers and Teachers

This book helps children grow by letting them practice reading. Here are a few guiding questions to help the reader build his or her comprehension skills. Possible answers appear here in red.

Before Reading

- **What do I think this book is about?** I think this book is about how fast dragster cars can go. I think this book is about the people who love to drive dragsters.
- **What do I want to learn about this topic?** I want to learn more about how a dragster slows down after a race. I want to learn how fast a dragster can go.

During Reading

- **I wonder why...** I wonder why dragsters are so loud. I wonder why Funny Cars cannot be older than 5 years old to race.
- **What have I learned so far?** I have learned that Top Fuel dragsters race side-by-side at over 300 miles (483 km) per hour. I have learned that dragsters race down a 1,000-foot (305-m) straight track.

After Reading

- **What details did I learn about this topic?** I have learned rear engine racers use fuel that is called nitromethane. I have learned that exhaust flames can get as hot as 7,000°F (3,871°C).
- **Read the book again and look for the glossary words.** I see the word *horsepower* on page 14, and the word *traction* on page 17. The other glossary words are found on page 23.

Library and Archives Canada Cataloguing in Publication

CIP available at Library and Archives Canada

Library of Congress Cataloging-in-Publication Data

CIP available at Library of Congress

Crabtree Publishing Company
www.crabtreebooks.com 1–800–387–7650

Print book version produced jointly with Blue Door Education in 2022

Written by: Craig Stevens

Print coordinator: Katherine Berti

Printed in the U.S.A./CG20210915/012022

PHOTO CREDITS:
istock.com, shutterstock.com, dreamstime.com. COVER: Elisa Putti | Dreamstime.com; Checkered flag used throughout ©N1chEZ | Shutterstock.com; Pages 2-3: ©Danny Raustadt | Dreamstime.com; Pages 4-5: GSenkow | Creative Commons Attribution-Share Alike 3.0 Unported; Pages 6-7: ©Danny Raustadt | Dreamstime.com, Kts | Dreamstime.com, ©Danny Raustadt | Dreamstime.com; Pages 8-9: ©Danny Raustadt | Dreamstime.com; Pages 10-11: ©Danny Raustadt | Dreamstime.com, Danny Raustadt | Dreamstime.com; Pages 12-13: ©Macleoddesigns | Dreamstime.com, ©Tkpphotography | Dreamstime.com, shutterstock.com/ Grindstone Media Group, Walter Arce | Dreamstime.com; Pages 14-15: ©Danny Raustadt | Dreamstime.com, ©Steve Mann | Dreamstime.com; Pages 18-19: ©Danny Raustadt | Dreamstime.com, © Steve Mann | Dreamstime.com; Pages 20-21: ©Danny Raustadt | Dreamstime.com, shutterstock.com | Action Sports Photography, ©Walter Arce | Dreamstime.com; Pages 22-23: ©Stahlkocher | GNU -Creative Commons Attribution-Share Alike 3.0 Unported

Published in the United States
Crabtree Publishing
347 Fifth Ave.
Suite 1402-145
New York, NY 10016

Published in Canada
Crabtree Publishing
616 Welland Ave.
St. Catharines, Ontario
L2M 5V6